A Note to Parents

DK READERS is a compelling program for beginning readers, designed in conjunction with leading literacy experts, including Dr. Linda Gambrell, Distinguished Professor of Education at Clemson University. Dr. Gambrell has served as President of the National Reading Conference, the College Reading Association, and the International Reading Association.

Beautiful illustrations and superb full-color photographs combine with engaging, easy-to-read stories to offer a fresh approach to each subject in the series. Each DK READER is guaranteed to capture a child's interest while developing his or her reading skills, general knowledge, and love of reading.

The five levels of DK READERS are aimed at different reading abilities, enabling you to choose the books that are exactly right for your child:

Pre-level 1: Learning to read
Level 1: Beginning to read
Level 2: Beginning to read alone
Level 3: Reading alone
Level 4: Proficient readers

The "normal" age at which a child begins to read can be anywhere from three to eight years old. Adult participation through the lower levels is very helpful for providing encouragement, discussing storylines, and sounding out unfamiliar words.

No matter which level you select, you can be sure that you are helping your child learn to read, then read to learn!

LONDON, NEW YORK, MUNICH,
MELBOURNE, AND DELHI

Editor Shari Last
Designer Mark Richards
Jacket Designer Lauren Rosier
Design Manager Ron Stobbart
Publishing Manager Catherine Saunders
Art Director Lisa Lanzarini
Publisher Simon Beecroft
Publishing Director Alex Allan
Production Editor Marc Staples
Production Controller Melanie Mikellides
Reading Consultant Dr. Linda Gambrell

First published in the United States in 2012
by DK Publishing
375 Hudson Street
New York, New York 10014
10 9 8 7 6 5
LEGO and the LEGO Logo are trademarks of The LEGO Group.
Copyright © 2012 The LEGO Group.
Produced by Dorling Kindersley
under license from The LEGO Group.

005—185327—May/12

DK books are available at special discounts when purchased in bulk for
sales promotions, premiums, fund-raising, or educational use.
For details, contact:
DK Publishing Special Markets
375 Hudson Street
New York, New York 10014
SpecialSales@dk.com

A catalog record for this book is available
from the Library of Congress.

ISBN: 978-0-7566-9528-6 (Paperback)
ISBN: 978-0-7566-9529-3 (Hardcover)

Color reproduction by Media Development and Printing, UK
Printed and bound by L-Rex Printing Co., Ltd, China

Discover more at
www.dk.com
www.LEGO.com

Contents

DK READERS

READING 3 ALONE

LEGO HERO FACTORY

HEROES IN ACTION

Written by Shari Last

Makuhero City Heroes

The Hero Factory makes brave robot heroes 24 hours a day, 7 days a week, 365 days a year. Each hero is powered by a Hero Core, a unique device that brings the hero's metal body to life.

The most famous group of heroes is Team Alpha. They are led by the tough, no-nonsense hero Preston Stormer. The other members of Team Alpha are Bulk, Rocka, Breez, Nex, Surge, Evo, Furno, and Stringer.

Rocka

Natalie Breez

Dunkan Bulk

Preston Stormer

Famous factory

Makuhero City is an enormous city, which is built up around the famous Hero Factory. The factory rises like a skyscraper at the center of the city.

After many missions together, Stormer has a lot of trust in his team.

The heroes of Makuhero City are built for a single purpose: to capture villains.

Jimi Stringer

Julius Nex

Mark Surge

Nathan Evo

William Furno

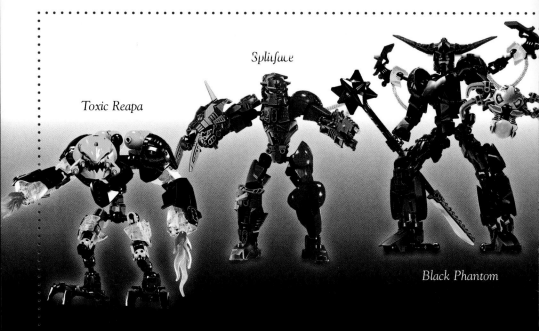

Toxic Reapa

Splitface

Black Phantom

Dangerous Foes

Across the universe, hundreds of dangerous robot villains put people's lives in danger. They know that sooner or later the heroes will hear about this and try to stop them—but they don't care!

Usually the heroes are able to capture a villain without too much trouble. However, some villains are cunning and manage to escape.

Core Hunter

XT4

Speeda Demon

Voltix

Jawblade

Thornraxx

Among the heroes' most dangerous enemies are Toxic Reapa, Splitface, Black Phantom, Core Hunter, XT4, Speeda Demon, Voltix, Jawblade, and Thornraxx.

The only thing these villains like more than committing a crime is escaping from a hero!

Villains in Cages

Whenever a hero defeats a villain, the prisoner is brought back to the Hero Factory. The captured villain is locked in a cell in the Villain Storage Unit, deep in the basement of the Hero Factory.

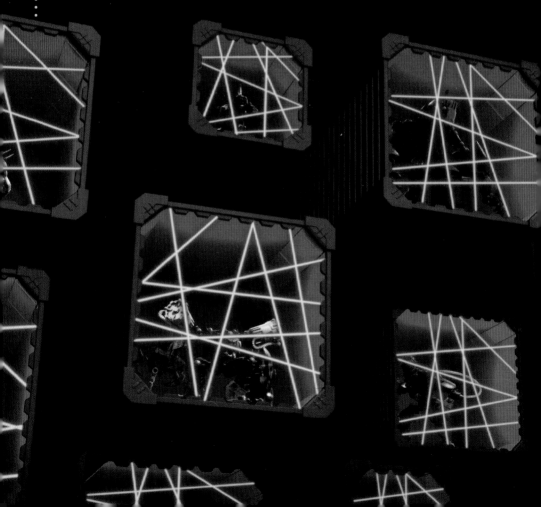

Each villain has his or her own cell, which is guarded by a red, glowing energy field.

Furno and Rocka have just secured the captured villain Voltix in his cell. No villain has ever escaped from the Hero Factory. Until now…

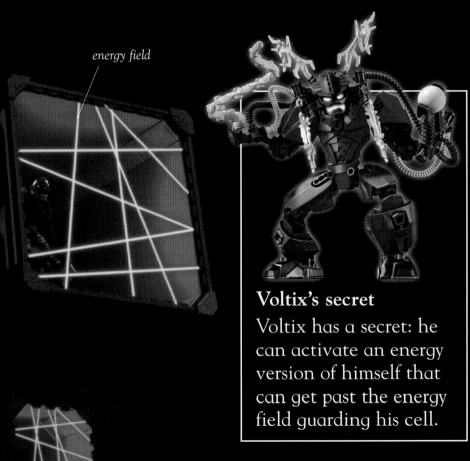

energy field

Voltix's secret
Voltix has a secret: he can activate an energy version of himself that can get past the energy field guarding his cell.

Escape of the Villains

Voltix has found a way to shut down the energy field guarding the villains' cells. He's also opened a Black Hole in the middle of the Hero Factory!

The villains don't waste any time. They are delighted to be free.

Black Hole
The Black Hole creates a passageway to another part of the universe. When the villains enter the Black Hole, they are transported away from the Hero Factory.

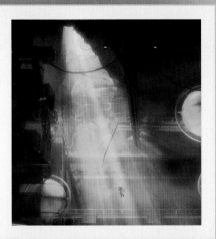

All of the dangerous robots jump down from their cells and run into the Black Hole.

The heroes try to stop the villains, but there are just too many of them. They all escape. This is the biggest disaster Hero Factory has ever faced!

Missions Assigned

Welcome to the Hero Factory's Mission Briefing Room. It is full of high-tech equipment, powerful weapons, and everything else the heroes need for their missions. There is even a villain tracking system, which finds the villains wherever they are.

After the mass breakout from the Villain Storage Unit, all the heroes gather in the Mission Briefing Room. Zib, the Mission Manager, assigns each hero a villain to capture. He also upgrades the heroes with new armor, weapons, or vehicles to help them on their missions.

Zib and Quadal
Zib and his floating assistant Quadal are programmed to manage the heroes and their missions. They are very clever, but have not been trained in battle.

Speeding Stormer

Team Alpha leader Stormer has been chosen to recapture Speeda Demon, a superfast villain who has escaped to the icy planet Kollix IV.

Stormer's armor is upgraded to an XL version and he is issued a new plasma gun, which has an ultra-powerful bolt shooter. He also gets an Ultramach speedcycle to keep up with Speeda Demon.

Hero Pod

The heroes pilot a spaceship called a Hero Pod to travel to different planets on their missions. There are hundreds of these in the Hero Pod Launch Facility, ready and waiting to transport a hero wherever he needs to go!

Stormer is fearless and he cannot wait to come to face-to-face with his new foe. He heads to the Hero Pod Launch Facility, where he boards a Hero Pod and takes off on his mission.

Full Speed Ahead

On Kollix IV, Stormer steers his speedcycle through sharp twists and turns. Up ahead is Speeda Demon, riding his own bike. The ice canyons of Kollix IV are dangerous and slippery, but Stormer can handle it!

Just when Speeda Demon thinks he is getting away, Stormer releases his brand new hero cuffs.

Hero cuffs
Each hero has a pair of hero cuffs. They are made from a superstrong material. The cuffs find the nearest villain, cuff him, and take away his powers.

They attach themselves to Speeda Demon's wrists and he crashes his bike. Stormer is victorious!

Underwater Furno

Furno is still a hero-in-training (also known as a rookie), but he is ready to go on a mission alone. Zib sends Furno to the underwater world of Scylla, where the shark-like villain Jawblade is hiding.

Jawblade might be at home in the water, but Furno will be more than a match for him with his new, high-tech Aquajet pack and deadly plasma gun. The plasma gun is designed to work underwater without electrocuting the hero it is attached to. Lucky for Furno!

Ready for action
The world of Scylla is dark and strange, but Furno is confident. He has the skills to complete his mission!

Aquajet pack

plasma gun

Catch of the Day

Underwater on Scylla, Furno finally finds Jawblade. The swimming villain uses his magma blades to send blasts of volcanic energy at Furno, but the hero uses his Aquajet pack to dodge them with ease.

Look out! Jawblade has found a rare mineral called Oxidium on the seabed. It makes things rust quickly.

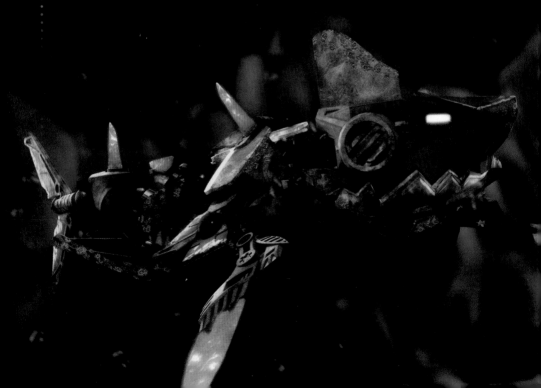

Jawblade throws some Oxidium at Furno and the hero's metal body rusts over in seconds.

Furno can't move at all, but he won't be defeated that easily. He activates his Hero Core and the rust disappears. Jawblade is shocked and Furno uses the moment to catch him and cuff him. Mission complete!

Anti-Toxic Evo

Evo is a new rookie member of Team Alpha, but he is also ready for battle! Zib sends him to chase Toxic Reapa through the dense jungles of Z'Chaya.

Toxic Reapa was born on Z'Chaya, so he feels right at home! He is armed with a tank of toxic waste that melts anything it touches, making him a very dangerous villain indeed.

A poisonous villain
Toxic Reapa has no conscience. He shoots poison at whoever stands in his way.

Zib is always prepared, so he equips Evo with anti-toxic armor and a tank arm that can resist Toxic Reapa's poison. Evo is ready to go. He boards his Hero Pod and heads toward Z'Chaya.

tank arm

hero cuffs

Rookie Does Good

Rookie Evo is having a tough time keeping track of Toxic Reapa. The sneaky villain knows his way around Z'Chaya so well that Evo keeps losing him. Evo shoots at Toxic Reapa with his blaster, but the villain keeps jumping out of the way.

Jungle planet
The jungles of Z'Chaya are full of thick trees and secret caves. Toxic Reapa thinks he has the advantage. But does he?

Evo needs a new strategy, so he decides to trust his instincts. When he finally spots Toxic Reapa scurrying up a tree trunk, Evo fires his blaster behind him. The power of the blast pushes him through the air and... CRUNCH! He knocks Toxic Reapa to the ground.

Before Toxic Reapa can fire his poison, Evo has him cuffed. Another villain is captured!

Surge in Zero Gravity

Surge is the youngest member of Team Alpha, but he is very confident. Zib sends Surge to the Sigma Sigma Communications Satellite, which is surrounded by a zero-gravity asteroid field. His task: capture Splitface.

duo-plated armor

Electricity shooter

The dangers of outer space

The Sigma Sigma Communications Satellite is located in an asteroid field in outer space. There is no gravity here, so the robots must be careful not to float away into space.

Splitface is a half-mad villain who likes to talk to himself—but Surge is not afraid. He has duo-plated armor, which can withstand the atmosphere in outer space. He also wears a pair of alpha-magnetic gravity boots so he doesn't float away into zero-gravity.

Surge is also armed with an Electricity shooter, which means that Splitface had better look out!

Caught and Cuffed

Splitface has a split personality, which means he thinks he is two different people. Although he is unbalanced, it also means he can attack with the strength of two people instead of one! Poor Surge is finding it difficult to fight back.

Crazy villain
Splitface is half mechanical, half organic. He can never decide on anything.

Luckily, Surge is equipped with the best weapons in the universe. During a battle on an asteroid, Surge uses his Electricity shooter to fry his foe's circuits. Splitface drifts off into the asteroid field... until Surge catches him in a pair of hero cuffs. Now Splitface isn't going anywhere!

Stringer Gets Serious

Stringer sometimes makes jokes, even during a dangerous mission. However, this relaxed hero knows that his latest mission is no joke. He must recapture Voltix, the energy-shooting criminal who freed all the villains in the first place!

Sonic blaster
Stringer's weapon is a quad-amplitude mega-decibel sonic blaster. It shoots sound waves!

Stringer is instructed to follow the deadly Voltix to his hideout on the planet Tansari VI. Tansari VI is a dark, misty planet that crackles with bolts of lightning. Before Stringer can capture Voltix, he must first find him…

A Deadly Threat

Black Phantom is a genius villain. He is taller and tougher than most other villains—and smarter, too!

razor saber staff

Arachnix

Black Phantom secretly masterminded the breakout from the Hero Factory. He wants to distract the heroes so he can enter the factory and carry out his own evil plan.

While the heroes race off on their missions, Black Phantom makes his way to the center of the Hero Factory. He unleashes a unique weapon: an evil drone called Arachnix. Arachnix looks like a robot spider. He can make clones of himself that scurry off to all corners of the factory.

Creepy Arachnix
Arachnix is loyal to his master Black Phantom. His clones are identical copies of himself, all ready to do Black Phantom's bidding!

An Evil Plan

Black Phantom makes his way to the Mission Briefing Room where he finds Zib, the Mission Manager.

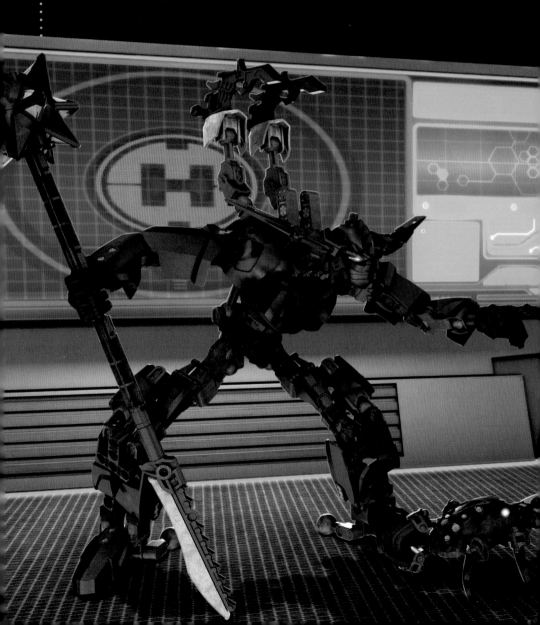

He forces Zib to shut down the factory and activate the protective energy shield. Now the returning heroes won't be able to get back in!

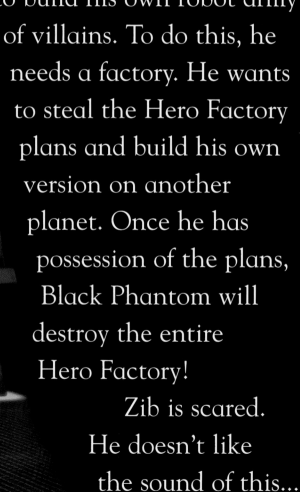

Black Phantom reveals his plan: he wants to build his own robot army of villains. To do this, he needs a factory. He wants to steal the Hero Factory plans and build his own version on another planet. Once he has possession of the plans, Black Phantom will destroy the entire Hero Factory!

Zib is scared. He doesn't like the sound of this...

energy shield

crossbow

reinforced
armor

Last Remaining Hero

Rocka is Team Alpha's newest member. The rookie is not as experienced as the other heroes, so he has stayed behind to guard the Hero Factory while the others complete their missions.

Armed with a crossbow and energy shield, Rocka is not afraid of danger. But when he notices that Hero Factory has been locked down, he becomes suspicious.

Rocka contacts Zib to find out what is going on, but Zib is being threatened by Black Phantom. Zib says that it is just a false alarm, but Rocka is not convinced. He might be a rookie, but he knows something is not right!

Factory Chase

Rocka has discovered what is really going on in the Hero Factory. Black Phantom is on the loose, and he must be stopped!

The Hero Assembly Tower is a tall chamber at the heart of the Hero Factory. It is full of platforms and machines that assemble the new robot heroes.

Black Phantom has found the Hero Factory plans and now he is almost at the top of the tower. Who knows what damage he will cause when he reaches the summit!

Rocka uses all of his skill to climb the tower, but he is chased by hundreds of Arachnix clones. He must catch Black Phantom. The fate of the Hero Factory depends on it!

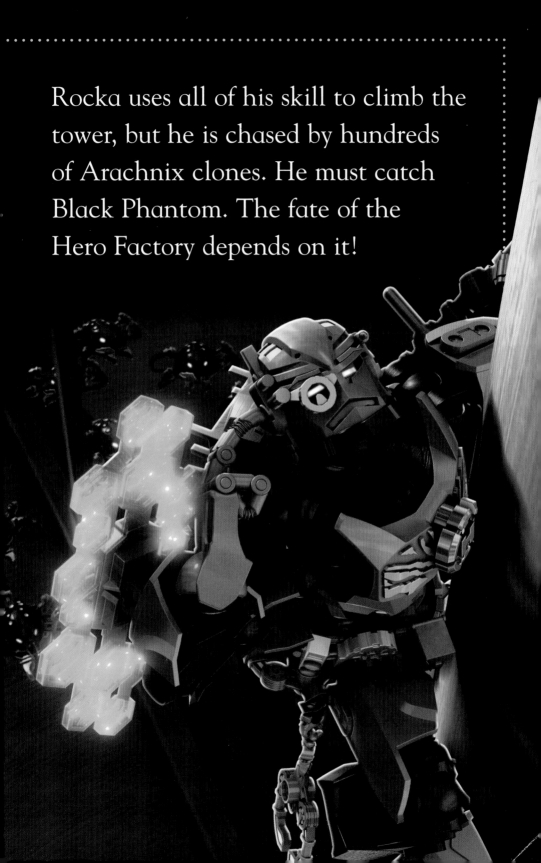

Battle in the Tower

Stormer, Furno, Surge, and Evo have completed their missions. They arrive back at the Hero Factory, but the energy shield is up. They cannot land!

Rocka uses the communications system to deactivate the shield.

The heroes rush to meet him at the Hero Assembly Tower. They are just in time! They fire their blasters at the terrifying Arachnix clones, slowly defeating the drones one by one. Thanks to his team, Rocka is free to go after Black Phantom.

Power Overload

At the very top of the tower, Black Phantom has plugged himself into the cables that power the entire factory. He is going to overload the power source and destroy the whole factory!

Rocka finally catches up to the villain. While they battle, Stormer tells Rocka to cut Black Phantom loose from the cables. However, Evo has another idea. The rookie has learned to trust his instincts. He thinks it's a better idea to plug even more cables into Black Phantom. What should Rocka do?

All the heroes agree with Evo—
even Stormer. So Rocka plugs more
and more cables into Black Phantom.
The villain vibrates and his power
overloads. His circuits begin to fry!
The heroes win!

Latecomer

As the heroes congratulate each other and send Black Phantom down to the Villain Storage Unit, they realize someone is missing: Stringer. Whatever happened to him?

Suddenly the hero turns up, ready to help save the day.

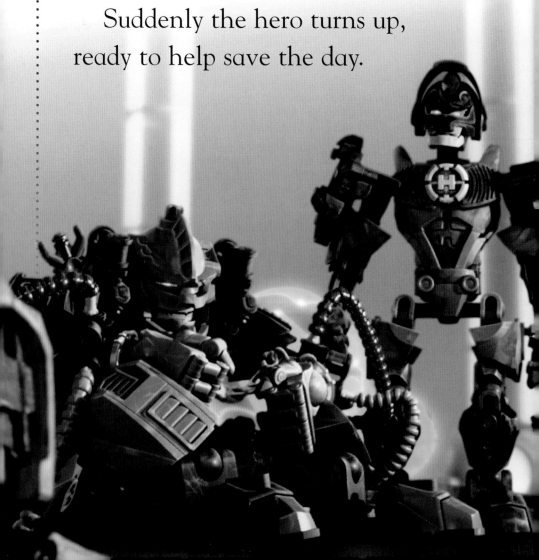

What took Stringer so long?

Well, after he captured Voltix on Tansari VI, he was ready to return to the Hero Factory, but he ran into a problem… he forgot where he parked his Hero Pod!

The End?

The crisis is over! The villains are back in their cells, and all the heroes have returned safely. Black Phantom is imprisoned in the Villain Storage Unit and the Hero Factory is secure once more.

Zib and the heroes check the factory for damage. Everything looks good at first, but they soon realize that one data file has been sent to an unknown location. What file is it? Where has it been sent? The heroes do not know.

Somewhere in the universe, an unknown villain has received a data file sent from the Hero Factory.

It contains the plans for the entire Hero Factory. The heroes may have won this battle, but there is a larger war coming…

Glossary

Assign
To give someone a job.

Asteroid field
An area of outer space that is filled with huge pieces of rock, known as asteroids.

Black Hole
A hole in outer space that acts like a passageway from one place to another.

Canyon
A deep valley between two steep cliff walls.

Circuit
A group of wires through which electricity can flow.

Clone
An identical copy of something.

Data
Information.

Deactivate
To turn something off, often by shutting the power down.

Device
An item made for a special purpose.

Drone
A robot-like machine that cannot think on its own.

Electrocute
To injure someone using electricity.

Energy field
An area of energy that surrounds something.

Energy shield
A shelter made of energy, which protects a building or a place.

Hero Assembly Tower
The tallest tower in the Hero Factory, where the robot heroes are created.

Hero Core
A small device that is placed inside each hero, bringing him or her to life. Each Hero Core is unique and influences the hero's personality.

Hero Factory
An organization that builds robot heroes to protect the universe.

Hero cuffs
A pair of handcuffs that attach themselves to the nearest villain and deactivate his powers.

Hero Pod
A spaceship that heroes fly on their missions.

Hero Pod Launch Facility
A chamber at the top of the Hero Factory where the Hero Pods are kept. It also has a launch pad, where the Hero Pods take off from.

Instinct
A gut feeling.

Mission Briefing Room
A room in the Hero Factory from where the heroes' missions are managed.

Mission Manager
A Hero Factory employee who remains at the factory and directs the heroes' on their missions.

Organic
Made of living material.

Oxidium
A rare substance that causes metal to rust very quickly.

Rookie
A new member of a team or organization.

Satellite
A mechanical object that floats in outer space collecting information.

Sound waves
The way that sound travels through the air.

Summit
The top.

Team Alpha
An elite team of heroes who work together on missions.

Toxic waste
Poisonous materials.

Zero-gravity
A place where objects float in the air because there is no gravity.